Robyn

the Christmas Party

Fairy

Special thanks to Rachel Elliot

First published in the United Kingdom in 2017 by Orchard U.K., Carmelite House, 50 Victoria Embankment, London EC4Y 0DZ.

ISBN 978-1-338-20709-5

10 9 8 7 6 5 4 3 2 1   18 19 20 21 22

Printed in the U.S.A.   40
First edition, October 2018

Robyn

the Christmas Party

Fairy

by Daisy Meadows

SCHOLASTIC INC.

The Fairyland Palace

Barn
Elf's Cottage

Clock Tower

Kirsty's House

Wetherbury Village

Jack Frost's Ice Castle

Town Hall

High St.

Come goblins from both far and near.
It's time to ruin the Christmas cheer.
Instead of parties, games, and fun,
Bring tears and groans to everyone!

The fairies and their human friends
Think that they can make amends.
But Christmas parties will all be
Filled with despair and misery!

Find the hidden letters in the stars throughout this book. Unscramble all 5 letters to spell a special holiday word!

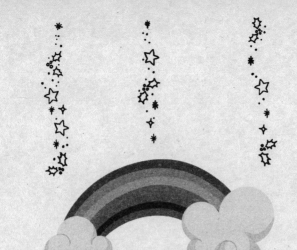

The Magic Christmas Cracker

Contents

Crazy Crackers

"I've never seen frost look so beautiful," said Rachel Walker, gazing out of the Town Hall window.

"It's a perfect Christmas Eve morning," agreed her best friend, Kirsty Tate, as she joined Rachel at the window.

The bright winter sun made everything outside the window sparkle. Kirsty's

1

hometown, Wetherbury, looked as if it had been covered with glittery white icing. The girls and their families were spending Christmas there together this year.

"The party tonight is going to be amazing." Rachel smiled. "And helping organize it makes everything even more fun!"

She turned around, watching the preparations going on all over the hall. Lots of people from the community had come together to throw a special Christmas party. The girls and their families were thrilled! The food and decorations were looking wonderful, but the highlight of the party was definitely going to be a beautiful ballet performance.

Mrs. Tate saw the girls by the window and smiled at them.

"Come on, you two, there's work to do!" she said. "We have a lot to finish before the party. Could you start setting the tables for the feast?"

Several long tables had been pushed together to make a big square in the center of the hall. Mrs. Tate gave the girls a cart piled high with tablecloths, place mats, napkins, silverware, and glasses.

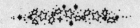

"Don't forget to put a Christmas cracker at each place setting," she said. "The crackers are in a box on the bottom of the cart. I can't wait to pull them apart at the party and see the toys inside!"

"I'm so excited about the Christmas party," said Rachel. "Just think, people all over the world are doing exactly the same thing we are right now—getting ready for Christmas."

"Not everyone!" said Kirsty. "At school, we've been learning about other holiday traditions from around the world, like Kwanzaa and Hanukkah, and how people celebrate Christmas in all different countries."

The girls worked quickly, laying out the bright-red tablecloths and beautiful

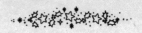

place settings. Soon the tables looked
very festive, with gold napkins
and sparkling glasses.

"Just one more thing
to do," said Rachel,
peering into the box.
"Time to put out
a cracker for each
guest!"

As she picked up one
of the crackers, it gave a loud
bang. Rachel squealed and dropped it.

"What's the matter?" cried Mrs. Tate,
hurrying over to the girls. "What
happened?"

"I'm OK! I was just surprised," said
Rachel. "This cracker went off all
by itself!"

"How strange," said Mrs. Tate, taking
the cracker and looking at it closely.
"It must be broken."

Suddenly, they heard another small
bang from inside the box.

"I've never had Christmas crackers that
went off by themselves before." Kirsty
frowned.

Mrs. Tate opened her mouth to reply,

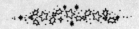

but just then one of the other volunteers groaned loudly.

"This tinsel isn't sparkly at all!" she said, holding up a long string of golden tinsel. "It's just dull. It looks terrible!"

"These decorations won't stay up, Mrs. Tate," called another volunteer from up on a ladder. "It doesn't seem to matter how many thumbtacks I use, they just fall down."

Mrs. Tate gave a heavy sigh and hurried off to deal with the new problems.

"Maybe I can figure out what's wrong," said Rachel, picking up the broken Christmas cracker. She peered into one end of it like a telescope and gave a little gasp. A beautiful little fairy was sitting cross-legged inside!

A Banned Band

The fairy waved at Rachel and zoomed out of the other end of the cracker. She was wearing a shimmering raspberry-colored party dress and a thin golden headband.

"Hello," she said. "I'm Robyn the Christmas Party Fairy."

"Hello, Robyn!" said the girls together.

"We should hide," added Rachel. "Quick, under here!"

The girls slipped under one of the party tables. The long tablecloth hid them completely.

"It's great to meet you, Robyn," said Kirsty. "But what are you doing here in Wetherbury?"

"Oh, girls, I need your help," cried Robyn, clasping her hands together. "Jack Frost has stolen my magic objects and I have to find them quickly, or else

Christmas parties everywhere will be
ruined!"

Rachel and Kirsty exchanged a
worried glance.

"What do you
mean?" Rachel
asked.

"It's my job to
make sure that
Christmas parties
in the human and
fairy worlds go well,"
Robyn explained. "Without
my objects, all the parties will be a holly
jolly mess."

"That's terrible!" said Kirsty. "We're
throwing a party here later, and
everyone's been working really hard to

get everything ready. It would be awful for it to go wrong."

"We're having a Christmas Eve party in Fairyland tonight, too," said Robyn. "There are supposed to be special performances from lots of amazing fairies."

"Was Jack Frost invited?" asked Rachel. "If he was left out, maybe that's why he stole your magic objects."

"Oh, he was invited," said Robyn. "But we didn't put his Gobolicious Band on the performance list, and he was very annoyed about that."

"What are your magic objects?" Rachel asked.

"My magic Christmas cracker symbolizes sharing, happiness, and feasting," said Robyn. "It makes sure that

there's plenty for everyone to eat and drink. My dancing shoes keep the party entertainment fun and exciting, and my magical snow globe brings the Christmas party spirit to every gathering."

"We'll help you find them before it's too late," said Kirsty, sounding determined.

"That's what I hoped you'd say," said Robyn, smiling. "If you come with me now, I can show you what Jack Frost has done in Fairyland."

Rachel and Kirsty both grinned. They knew that Robyn's magic

would make sure no one in the human world noticed they were gone, however long they spent in Fairyland.

Robyn gave a twirl, and her silky dress floated out around her as she raised her wand.

Then she said:

We wish to be in Fairyland
To see the party being planned.
We have to stop Jack Frost today
So take us there without delay!

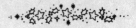

Tiny golden sparkles showered down over the girls, and they felt themselves shrinking. Wings unfurled from their shoulders, and they fluttered into the air beside Robyn.

Then there was a bright flash of light, and suddenly they were standing at the edge of a round ice rink, surrounded by

snowy fir trees. Isabelle the Ice Dance Fairy pirouetted around the beautiful ice rink.

Rachel, Kirsty, and Robyn had arrived in Fairyland!

Jack Frost on Ice

Rachel and Kirsty waved to Isabelle and skated over to her.

"Rachel! Kirsty!" said Isabelle, sounding excited. "It's great to see you! Are you here to help Robyn?"

"Yes," said Rachel. "It sounds like Jack Frost has been causing trouble again."

"Without Robyn's magic objects,

our performance might have to be canceled," said Isabelle sadly.

"Keep practicing," said Kirsty kindly. "We're not going to let Jack Frost ruin your party."

Robyn took the girls' hands. "Look over there," she said.

Among the fir trees, the girls could see the jumbled pieces of a broken, round stage. Behind it, a group of fairies were pointing their wands at a big Christmas tree. It seemed to be growing taller and taller.

"The Christmas Fairies have been

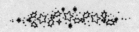

planning this party all year," said
Robyn. "That's a magic tree that was
supposed to tower
over the stage.
We've been
working on
spells to make
it grow its own
decorations
and gifts."

"It sounds
amazing!"
Rachel said
with a smile.

"But we really have to stop Jack Frost,
and fast," Robyn said, flicking back
her long brown hair. "Let me show you
what he did earlier today."

Robyn waved her wand over the ice

rink, and the frozen surface became glassy. Then pictures appeared in the ice! The girls saw Jack Frost marching into the glade. His cloak swirled around him, and three menacing goblins scurried along behind him.

Robyn was standing next to the stage, watching the Dance Fairies practice their routine.

"I'll make you sorry for leaving my amazing Gobolicious Band out of the

show!" Jack Frost yelled. "You silly
fairies always think things should go
your way, but I'm going to have the best
Christmas party in Fairyland—and your
party is going to FLOP!"

"Why do you have
to be so mean?"
asked Robyn.
"We've been
planning this
party for
months."

She picked
up a bag
that had
been next to her
feet. Jack Frost looked like he might
explode with anger.

"I can do anything I want!" he

21

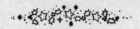

bellowed. "Especially with the help of some fairy magic!"

He pointed his wand at the bag in Robyn's hands. A bolt of blue lightning seemed to reach out and snatch it! Robyn yelped and tried to hold on to the bag, but Jack Frost's magic was too strong. He laughed loudly as the bag landed in his hands.

"Those things are mine!" cried Robyn. "I need them!"

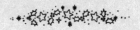

"WRONG!" Jack Frost shouted. "*I* need them! But until I'm ready to use them, I'm going to hide them somewhere so clever that you fairies will never find them!"

He handed the bag to his three goblins. Then he pointed his wand at them and chanted:

I know a Norwegian who likes to play pranks.
If he'll help trick the fairies, I'll give him my thanks.
Tiaras and tutus conceal a great prize,
And keep it away from those bright fairy eyes.
The treasure will lie in a Christmassy nook.

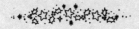

The very last place a fairy would look!

When Jack Frost spoke the last word, the bag and the goblins disappeared in a blinding flash. That same lightning bolt hit the stage and smashed it into pieces.

Then the picture in the ice melted away. Kirsty murmured the words of Jack Frost's spell under her breath.

"Do you have an idea?" Rachel asked her.

"I think that Jack Frost was being too clever for his own good," said Kirsty. "He used that spell to hide Robyn's magic objects, right?"

"Right," said Robyn and Rachel together.

"So the spell is full of clues that will tell

us where he hid the objects," said Kirsty. "We just have to figure out what they mean."

"But how are we going to do that?" asked Robyn.

Kirsty gave a little smile and raised her eyebrows. "I think I might know where to start," she said.

The Cottage in the Forest

"At school, we've been learning about different Christmas traditions around the world," Kirsty explained. "The first part of Jack Frost's spell said something about a Norwegian, didn't it?"

"Yes," said Robyn, repeating the words out loud.

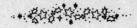

"I know a Norwegian who likes to play pranks.

If he'll help trick the fairies, I'll give him my thanks."

"In Norway, there's an elf who plays tricks on people at Christmastime," said Kirsty. "He watches over the animals on farms, as long as the farmers leave him bowls of porridge and leftovers from their Christmas meals. If they don't leave him food, he causes trouble for them."

"I know him!" Robyn exclaimed. "He's called the Barn Elf."

"Robyn, can you bring us to him?" asked Rachel.

Robyn nodded. "He lives in a distant

28

part of Fairyland," she said. "It will take us a little while to fly there."

"Then let's get started," said Rachel. "There's no time to waste!"

Soon the girls were flying beside Robyn, high above the green meadows of Fairyland. The toadstool houses and neat pathways slowly gave way to heather-covered hills and fields filled

with wildflowers. After what felt like
a long time, Robyn pointed to a dark
green forest just below them.

"We'll have to go in there," she said.
"The Barn Elf lives in the middle of the
Magic Forest."

They swooped down and darted in
between the tall, straight tree trunks. In
the forest, it seemed
as dark as night.
Very little light
could filter through
the thick leaves.

"We've never
been to this part
of Fairyland
before," said Kirsty,
looking around as
they flew along.

There were no fairies fluttering around here. Suddenly, Kirsty saw a pair of enormous eyes blinking right at her from behind a big branch. Yikes!

"Don't be scared," said Robyn. "There are lots of magic creatures in this forest, but they only live here because they're shy."

A pink plume of smoke coiled under their noses, and the girls smelled a wonderful aroma.

"Mmm, it smells like coffee and toast," said Rachel.

"There are all sorts of mysterious kinds of magic in this forest," said Robyn.

"Listen!" said Kirsty.

In a clearing up ahead, they could hear a gruff voice humming a folk tune. Robyn gave a little smile.

"That's the Barn Elf," she said.

The three friends fluttered slowly to the forest floor. Old leaves crackled under their feet as they landed in the clearing.

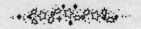

A neat garden surrounded a small, white cottage with a red roof. A ladder was leaning against the side of the house, and a bucket sat at the foot of it.

"The humming's coming from the other side of the house," said Rachel. "Come on, let's fly around."

The friends fluttered behind the house. The back door was open, leading into a cozy-looking kitchen. A small elf was

standing on the back doorstep, sipping
a hot drink from a mug and rubbing
his back with one hand. He had a long
white beard that reached almost to his
feet, and he was wearing
gray pants and a gray
tunic. The only
colorful thing
about him was
his bright-red hat.
Rachel and Kirsty
smiled at him, and
saw that his beady
eyes were sparkling
and sharp.

"Well, well, well," he said. "What
brings three little fairies all the way to
the Magic Forest?"

"Hello, Barn Elf," said Robyn,

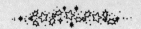

hovering in front of him. "We came here looking for you."

The Barn Elf raised his eyebrows, and his beard twitched as if he was wiggling his chin.

"How surprising!" he said. "What could the fairies want from me?"

"We were wondering if Jack Frost came to see you, and if you know anything about the magic objects he stole from Robyn," said Kirsty.

The Barn Elf paused as if he was thinking hard. It seemed to the girls that his eyes twinkled even more brightly.

"Jack Frost, huh?" he asked. "Well, not to be rude, but why should I tell you that?"

Despite his words, he sounded friendly, but the girls were taken aback.

"Out of the goodness of your heart?"
Kirsty suggested. "Robyn really needs
your help."

The Barn Elf chuckled.

"I'm not loyal to anyone," he said,
"but I sometimes give Jack Frost a
helping hand. You see, I like pranks and
tricks. And Jack Frost's very good at
making mischief. But King Oberon and

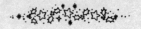

Queen Titania of Fairyland don't like that mischief as much as I do."

"But this isn't just mischief," Rachel pleaded. "Without Robyn's magic objects, the Fairyland Christmas party will be ruined! If you know anything, please help us."

The Barn Elf swigged down the last of his drink and groaned as he rubbed his back again.

"It makes no difference to me if the fairy party happens or not," he said. "If you need something from me, you'll have to think of a way to make me *want* to help you."

"How can we do that?" Robyn asked.

The Barn Elf chuckled again. "That's for you to figure out!" he said.

The Cracker Hunt

Kirsty and Robyn looked at each other gloomily. It seemed like the Barn Elf was determined not to help them. But as Rachel kept watching, she saw him rub his back again.

"Did you hurt yourself?" she asked kindly.

"I've been cleaning the cottage windows," said the Barn Elf. "But I strained my poor old back when I was reaching up."

Rachel remembered seeing the ladder and bucket in front of the cottage. Suddenly, she had an idea.

"If we clean the windows for you, will you tell us what you know about Robyn's magic objects?" she asked.

The Barn Elf smiled.

"Now that is what I call a fair deal," he said. "I'll do it! But only if you don't use magic to clean the windows."

Robyn waved her wand and gave each of them some small cloths and a bucket full of hot, soapy water. They flew around the cottage and washed all the glass. Then they polished the windows

until they sparkled like diamonds. The
Barn Elf sat on a three-legged wooden
stool and watched them work with a
big smile on his face.

When they finished, he nodded and
beckoned to them. Robyn made the
buckets and cloths vanish with one
flick of her magic wand, and the fairies
flew down and landed in front of the
Barn Elf.

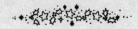

"Thank you," he said. "You've saved me a lot of work. In return, I'll tell you what I know. Earlier today, a Christmas cracker arrived here in the mail. It was addressed to Jack Frost, care of the Barn Elf."

"That must be my magic cracker!" Robyn exclaimed.

"I bet Jack Frost sent it here himself, hoping that you would keep it safe," said Kirsty.

"That's what I thought," said the Barn Elf, nodding. "But as I explained before, I'm not loyal to anyone. I don't obey the fairies, and I don't obey Jack Frost."

"So may we have the Christmas cracker back?" asked Rachel.

The Barn Elf looked at her, his eyes gleaming with mischief.

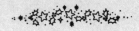

"I only promised to tell you what I knew," he said. "But I'm very glad to have clean windows, so if you can find the cracker, you can keep it."

The three fairy friends exchanged determined glances.

"May we search your cottage?" asked Robyn.

"Be my guests," the Barn Elf said with a chuckle.

A great hunt began! The fairies fluttered, darted, and zoomed through the rooms of the little cottage. They peered under cushions, opened

cupboards, and crept behind furniture, but it was no use. Robyn's magical Christmas cracker was nowhere to be seen.

At last, they returned to the living room and sat down in front of the fire, tired and disappointed.

It was a warm, Christmassy room with a glimmering tree, garlands along the walls, and a stocking hanging over the

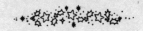

cozy fireplace. The table in the corner was set for Christmas dinner.

"Maybe it's not in the cottage at all," said Robyn. "The Barn Elf could have hidden it anywhere in the forest."

"Or he could be carrying it right now," Kirsty suggested.

But Rachel shook her head.

"I don't think he would have left it in the forest," she said. "And his clothes don't have any pockets. I'm sure it's here, but he's sneaky. He's hidden it somewhere very clever."

"Yes," said Robyn, sounding baffled. "Jack Frost's spell talked about hiding things in a Christmassy nook. Maybe it's tucked in a small cubbyhole somewhere and we'll never find it."

"We'll find it," said Rachel, squeezing the fairy's hand.

The girls thought hard. Then Kirsty gave a little laugh.

"Where's the best place to hide something?" she asked. "In with lots of other things that are exactly the same! And where do you find lots of Christmas crackers?"

"On the dining table!" shouted Robyn and Rachel together.

The three of them zoomed over to the Barn Elf's little dining table. There was a box of six crackers on the end of the table.

Five of them looked exactly the same,
but the sixth cracker was pink and
yellow, and was glittering with sparkles
of fairy dust.

"My magic cracker!" Robyn
exclaimed. "We found it!"

She picked it up and it instantly shrank
to fairy-size. The girls quickly flew out
of the cottage and found the Barn Elf

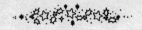

still sitting on his little stool. He smiled when he saw Robyn holding her magic cracker.

"Nice job," he said.

"It was a good hiding place," said Kirsty. "We had fun trying to find it!"

"It's been very interesting to meet you all," replied the Barn Elf. "I'll have to thank Jack Frost for arranging it."

He chuckled again, and Robyn turned to the girls.

"You've been

wonderful," she said. "I'm going to send you home now, because I have to return my magic cracker to its rightful place. But I'll come and get you later to look for the other objects, if that's OK?"

Kirsty and Rachel exchanged a happy glance.

"Of course," said Rachel. "One down, two to go!"

The Dancing Shoes

Contents

Party Plans

Rachel and Kirsty returned to
Wetherbury in a swirl of fairy dust.
Thanks to Robyn's magic, no time
had passed in the human world while
they were away. They crept out from
where they had been hiding, and quickly
finished putting the Christmas crackers
on the table.

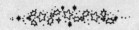

"No more crackers are going off by themselves, thank goodness," said Rachel with a smile.

"Yes, and all the problems with the Christmas decorations seem to be fixed," Kirsty added, looking around the hall. "It must be because we found Robyn's magic cracker."

Mrs. Tate walked over to the girls. "The tables look beautiful," she said. "Great job!"

"What else can we do to help?" asked Rachel happily.

"There are still lots of decorations to put up," Mrs. Tate replied. "Then the Christmas tree needs to be decorated, and there are balloons to blow up, too."

Rachel glanced up at the clock on the wall. It was almost lunchtime.

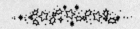

"We'd better get started!" she said.

The girls worked hard. They put ornaments and lights on the tree, hung paper chains across the room, and started to blow up the balloons. They only stopped for five minutes to eat some sandwiches that Mrs. Tate had made. Neither of them had a moment to think about Robyn or Jack Frost's spell.

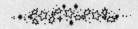

At three o'clock, Kirsty tied the last balloon and let out a long breath.

"I think we must have blown up hundreds of balloons," she said.

"I definitely think we've done enough," said Rachel, giggling.

They could hardly see the hall floor under all the bouncing balloons!

"I don't know what we would have

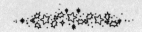

done without you
two," said Mrs.
Tate, looking
around.

"Can we do
anything else,
Mom?" Kirsty
asked.

"Well, the ballet
dancers are busy
rehearsing in the side room," said Mrs.
Tate, pointing to a closed door. "Why
don't you take a break and watch the
dancing? I might join you in a little
while."

The girls nodded eagerly. The
highlight of the party was going to be
a performance of the famous Christmas
party scene from *The Nutcracker*. The

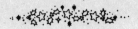

two friends loved ballet, so they couldn't wait to see it.

Rachel and Kirsty knocked on the door and went in. The room was filled with dancers in frilly, fancy costumes. The beautiful *Nutcracker* music was playing in the background, and the director was standing in the middle of the room. He was clutching his hair with both hands, looking frazzled.

Behind the dancers, the girls could see boxes wrapped to look like presents, a nutcracker doll, and a little white jewelry box.

"That's the doll that magically comes to life in the ballet," said Rachel, pointing to the nutcracker doll.

The girls smiled at each other. They knew all about magic, thanks to their

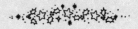

friendship with the fairies.

Just then, one of the dancers fell down, and three other ballerinas tripped over her. The music stopped.

"No, no, NO!" the director exclaimed. "You all knew these steps perfectly yesterday. What's the matter with you?"

The dancers gathered around the director and started arguing and trying to explain.

"It doesn't sound like rehearsals are going very well," said Kirsty under her breath.

"It must be because Robyn's dancing shoes are missing," said Rachel. "We *have* to get them back before the performance starts this afternoon."

"That means we have to solve the next part of Jack Frost's spell," Kirsty added. "If we don't, the fairy party will be ruined, too."

The girls had already solved the first two lines of the spell, but there were still four lines left to decipher.

Suddenly, Rachel noticed something.

The lid of the little jewelry box was open, and music had begun to play.

"Look, there's a tiny ballerina inside that jewelry box," she said.

Kirsty looked, and then gave her friend a big smile.

"That's not a ballerina, Rachel," she said. "That's Robyn!"

Mystery Ballerina

Robyn pirouetted into the air and zoomed toward the girls. She flew high over the heads of the dancers, but luckily none of them looked up. They were too busy worrying about the performance.

"Hi, Rachel and Kirsty," Robyn called out. "I'm here because I think the next part of the spell might have something to do with the dance at your party. It's a ballet, isn't it?"

"Yes," said Rachel. "What are the
words from the spell again?"

Robyn recited:

"*Tiaras and tutus conceal a great prize,
And keep it away from those bright*
fairy eyes."

"The rehearsals aren't going very
well," said Kirsty, pointing to
the arguing
dancers.
"I wonder
if Jack Frost
has hidden
your dancing
shoes here!"

"Time's
running
out," said
Robyn.

"If the magic dancing shoes are here, we have to find them soon. Without them, all Christmas party entertainment will be ruined. What a mess!"

"It would be easier to look around if we were fairies," Rachel said, winking at Robyn.

Robyn grinned, and in an instant the girls were fluttering in the air beside her on gauzy wings. The three friends split up and flew around the room, keeping an eye on the dancers below to make sure that no one spotted them.

A few minutes
later, they met
up again
behind the
jewelry box.

"Any
luck?" asked
Robyn.

"I saw lots of
candy wrappers on the floor over there,"
said Kirsty, pointing. "The dancers
wouldn't throw garbage around. Do you
think it could be a goblin?"

"They do like candy," Robyn agreed.
"And Jack Frost might have told a goblin
to guard the dancing shoes."

"One of the dancers lost her tutu,"
Rachel added. "I overheard her telling
the others about it."

Just then, the music started again. The director clapped his hands.

"Places, everyone!" he called. "Let's start from the beginning."

The dancers all hurried to their positions, and the scene began again.

Robyn and the girls fluttered behind a
curtain to watch. But once again, the
dancers forgot the steps.

"Hopeless!" cried the director.
"Absolutely hopeless! And the only
dancer who remembered all the steps is
dressed completely wrong. Why are you
wearing green tights?"

Rachel, Kirsty, and
Robyn exchanged
surprised glances
and peeked
around the
curtain. At the
end of a row
of dancers
was a short
ballerina in a
frilly pink tutu.

She had long, green legs and a pointy nose, but her dance steps were perfect.

"Oh my goodness," whispered Kirsty. "That's a goblin!"

Rachel gasped. "I think you're right!"

Disaster on the
Dance Floor

"Yes, and he has my dancing shoes," Robyn added. "Look!"

A tiny pair of silver ballet shoes was hanging around the goblin's neck on a little chain.

"He turned them into a charm," said Rachel, worried.

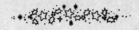

"That's why he can dance so well," said Robyn with a heavy sigh. "The magic from my dancing shoes is making him a spectacular dancer!"

They watched the goblin ballerina perform an elegant leap across the room. The director clapped his hands.

"Everyone, look at this! That's what you should all be doing!" he cried.

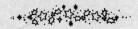

The goblin ballerina was soon hidden among a crowd of other dancers, who were trying to copy his steps.

"How are we going to get the dancing shoes away from him?" asked Kirsty.

Suddenly, Rachel gave a little smile and pointed across the rehearsal room.

"Someone else is trying to reach him, too," she said.

A plump goblin was hopping around the edge of the room, trying to talk to his goblin friend while hiding from the ballet dancers at the same time.

"Let's fly closer to him," Kirsty suggested.

"Maybe we can get near the other goblin by following him."

The three friends flew down and hovered behind the plump goblin. They could hear him muttering to himself.

"Why is he messing around with these silly dancers?" the goblin grumbled. "We have to get to the Ice Castle as quickly as possible, or Jack Frost won't be able to hold his dance competition."

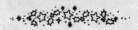

"Did you hear that?" whispered Rachel. "Jack Frost wants to use the magic dancing shoes for his own dance competition. We have to keep the goblins from taking them away!"

Just then, the music stopped again.

"This is a dance disaster!" cried the director. "It's all wrong! Start again!"

Kirsty pulled Rachel and Robyn behind the closest curtain. She turned to Robyn with sparkling eyes.

"Robyn, can you turn us into ballerinas?" she asked with a smile. "I have an idea!"

Robyn waved her wand, and instantly Rachel and Kirsty were transformed back to human-size. They stepped out from behind the curtain and looked at each other. Rachel was wearing a red

silk tutu, and Kirsty's outfit was made of yellow satin. Their hair was held up in buns with matching ribbons tied around them. Robyn hid herself in a fold of Rachel's tutu.

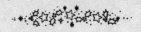

"These would be the best party dresses ever!" Rachel exclaimed.

"Come on," said Kirsty. "I think this is the only way to get close to the goblin ballerina. We have to dance!"

Pirouette Pile-up

Feeling very nervous, Rachel and Kirsty slipped in among the other dancers. Everyone was talking at once, and no one even noticed the two new ballerinas. Kirsty's heart was thumping so loudly she thought that everyone must be able to hear it.

"Come on," said Rachel, taking Kirsty's hand. "Let's find that goblin!"

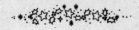

She pulled her best friend through the
crowd of dancers until
they reached the goblin
ballerina. He was
standing on
one toe shoe.
His other leg
stretched out
behind him,
and a tiara
hung crookedly
over one of his ears.

"He might recognize us," Kirsty
whispered. "We've met a lot of Jack
Frost's goblins before."

There was a small group of dancers to
the right of the goblin. Rachel led Kirsty
to the back of the group, keeping out of
the goblin's view.

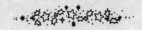

"If we can dance up behind him, we might be able to lift the charm from around his neck," said Kirsty.

"Places, please!" called the director, clapping his hands. "Hurry! We don't have much time!"

The beautiful music began to play again, and all the ballerinas took their places. Rachel and Kirsty each chose a dancer and tried to copy her movements. But the dancers all kept tripping and turning the wrong way! They stumbled over their own feet and landed with loud thumps instead of graceful steps. Soon the director was pulling on his own hair again.

"You sound like a herd of elephants!" He groaned.

The goblin pirouetted past the girls,

and the charm swung out toward Kirsty. She reached out to grab it, but the goblin had already twirled away.

"Arms up, and smile!" ordered the director. "This is a Christmas party scene, so you're all supposed to be dancing and looking happy."

The goblin gave a wide grin that looked more like a grimace. He whirled past Rachel, and she saw the dancing

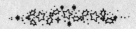

shoes charm shining on the chain. Her
heart thumped as she reached her hand
toward the charm. She felt it brush her
fingertips, but she couldn't hold on to it
as it flew past.

The girls danced on, following the
other dancers as well as they could. But
they kept tripping over their own feet.

"I'm being so clumsy!" Kirsty cried.

"It's because that greedy goblin ballerina is using all the magic from the dancing shoes for himself," Robyn whispered, looking up at her from the folds of Rachel's tutu.

Rachel stubbed her toe against a table.

"We have to get the charm back," she said, "or this dance will be a total disaster!"

The girls tried their best, but every time the goblin came close to them, the charm slipped out of their grasp. As the dance went on, Kirsty saw the door of the rehearsal room open. Then Mrs. Tate stuck her head into the room.

"Kirsty, it's your mom!" Rachel said in a low voice. "She must have come to watch the rehearsal!"

"But if she sees us dancing, she's going to say something," Kirsty whispered in alarm.

In her panic, she stopped dancing.

Suddenly, two other dancers crashed into her, and they all fell down in a heap. The goblin was mid-pirouette, and he squawked as he toppled sideways over the other dancers. Before anyone knew it, there was a pile of dancers in the middle of the room, with the goblin at the bottom.

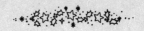

Kirsty found herself squished against the goblin's smelly feet!

"Help!" she cried, coughing and holding her nose. "Rachel! Please help me!" If she couldn't free herself, she'd end up squished by the goblin ballerina!

A Safe Pair of Shoes!

Kirsty wriggled and jiggled as hard as she could. Then she felt Rachel's hands grasping hers.

"Pull!" whispered Rachel.

As Kirsty was sliding out from underneath the pile of dancers, she spotted something silvery out of the corner of her eye. It was half hidden under a tutu, but it sparkled in the light.

"Rachel!" Kirsty exclaimed. "I can see the charm necklace!"

Kirsty lunged for the chain just as the goblin squirmed around and spotted her.

"My charm!" he squawked. "Get away from it!"

His long fingers grasped for the chain.  Kirsty stretched out her arm to try to reach it first. Then the plump goblin stuck his head into the pile between them.

"What's going on?" he snapped. "We have to get to the Ice Castle *now*!"

"I'm trapped!" wailed the ballerina goblin. "And I dropped the magic charm necklace!"

"You fool!" the plump goblin yelped. "Now those pesky girls are trying to get it before us."

"Quick, Kirsty!" cried Rachel.

With a determined stretch, Kirsty got her fingers to the chain at exactly the same moment as the plump goblin. They each grabbed it and pulled—and the dancing shoes flew off the chain and into the air!

Rachel caught them in one hand and tugged Kirsty out of the pile of dancers with the other. Then she looked up and saw Mrs. Tate heading their way.

"Your mom's coming!" said Rachel. "Let's go!"

The girls darted behind the curtain, and Robyn flew out of Rachel's tutu. Kirsty handed her the magic dancing shoes.

"Thank you so much!" the little fairy said, beaming. "You're wonderful friends." Tears of happiness sparkled in her eyes as the dancing shoes returned

to their proper size. With two taps of
Robyn's wand, Rachel and Kirsty were
back in their ordinary clothes. They
hugged each other in excitement.

"Hooray!
We did it!"
Kirsty cheered
in delight.

"You were
both amazing,"
said Robyn.
"I need to take
the dancing shoes
to Fairyland now,
but I'll be back really
soon. I still have to find my magic snow
globe before the parties start, and I know
I can't do it without you two."

She blew a kiss to each of the girls.

Then she disappeared in a little puff of fairy dust.

Kirsty nudged Rachel and they watched as the two goblins trudged out of the room, elbowing each other and scowling. One of them was still wearing his crooked tiara.

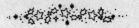

The girls shared a smile and slipped out from behind the curtain to join Mrs. Tate.

"Oh, hello, girls!" she said, hugging them. "I was so worried about the rehearsal that I didn't even see you."

"It looks like things are going better now," said Rachel happily.

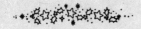

The ballerinas were dancing
beautifully, and the director was smiling.

"I wonder what Jack Frost will say
when he finds out that Robyn has two of
her magic objects back," said Rachel in a
low voice.

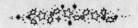

"I don't care what he says," said Kirsty. "I'm just happy that all performances at Christmas parties are safe again."

"I can't wait to see the ballet later," Rachel added with a giggle.

Kirsty put an arm around her best friend and gave her a squeeze.

"Me neither," she said. "It's going to be magical!"

The Snow Globe

Contents

An Exciting Idea

"We're finally ready for the party!" said
Kirsty, looking around the Town Hall.

The tables were covered with delicious
food, the tree was sparkling with lights
and ornaments, and garlands were looped
across the ceiling. Mrs. Tate pulled aside
the curtains and peered out the window.
Then she turned to Rachel and Kirsty
with a smile.

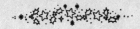

"The stars are out, the snow is falling, and Santa Claus has taken to the sky in his sleigh," she said.

"*And* it's time for the party to start!" added Rachel, giving a little skip of excitement.

She and Kirsty had worked very hard to help get ready for Wetherbury's Christmas party.

"I just hope that we have enough time to find Robyn's magic snow globe," Kirsty whispered.

They had found two of the three items that Jack Frost had stolen, but without her snow globe, Robyn wouldn't be able to fill Christmas parties with the Christmas party spirit. Jack Frost's mysterious spell held the clue to where they would find the globe. But so far, they hadn't been able to figure it out. Rachel and Kirsty were a little worried, but their excitement about the party was keeping them busy for now.

"It all starts in the town square," said Mrs. Tate, pulling on her coat. "The

carol singers will lead the procession
from the clock tower, through the town,
and back here for the party. We'd
better hurry up if we want to join
them!"

The girls eagerly bundled up in their
coats, hats, scarves, and gloves. Then
they hurried out to join the procession.

A crowd of people was watching the
carol singers underneath the clock tower.

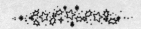

Each of them was
holding a lantern
or a sheet of music,
and they were
singing "Away
in a Manger."
A small band of
musicians played
behind them,
their instruments
shining in the
lantern light.

The snow was falling gently, and the girls drew in their breath.

"It's so pretty!" said Rachel in an awestruck whisper.

But just as she spoke, a gust of wind blew out one of the lanterns . . . then another . . . then another.

As some singers scrambled to relight their lanterns, the girls heard confused cries from the others.

"Where's my music sheet?"

"Mine's missing, too!"

"My music is all mixed up—what comes next?"

Suddenly, the trumpet let out a strange sound, and the girls heard muffled laughter from the crowd.

"This is all because Jack Frost still has the snow globe," whispered Kirsty. "If things keep going wrong, this party will turn into a joke."

"The procession is about to start," said Rachel. "Oh, Kirsty, we have to find the snow globe before everyone reaches the Town Hall. Otherwise, Jack Frost will ruin our party!"

The procession made its way out of the town square, and the girls stayed near the back, thinking hard. Mrs. Tate was chatting with some friends nearby. When the procession reached High Street, Rachel gave Kirsty's hand a squeeze.

"I just thought of something," she said. "Jack Frost's spell says that the snow globe is hidden 'where pesky fairies won't think to look,' remember?"

Kirsty nodded, looking interested.

"I was just thinking about how the Barn Elf hid the magic Christmas cracker in such an obvious place that we almost didn't think to look there," Rachel went on. "So where is the very last place that the fairies would look for something that was stolen *from* the magic glade? *In* the magic glade, of course!"

Kirsty's eyes opened very wide.

"I think you solved it!" she cried. "Oh, Rachel, we have to get to Fairyland right away!"

Rachel reached for the locket that hung around her neck. They had no time to lose!

A Search in Fairyland

After one of their first adventures with the fairies, Queen Titania had given the girls a wonderful present. They each had a special locket filled with fairy dust. If they ever urgently needed to see the fairies, all they had to do was open the lockets and sprinkle some fairy dust on themselves. They would instantly transform into fairies and be whisked

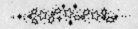

away to Fairyland! This time, there was just one tiny problem . . .

"How are we going to use our magic lockets without anyone seeing us?" Kirsty groaned.

High Street was filled with people following the procession, and Mrs. Tate kept turning around to check on the girls. Rachel looked around and frowned. All the stores were closed, and there were no alleyways or side streets to dart into while they transformed. They walked on, looking left and right to try to find somewhere they could hide.

Suddenly, there was a loud, clanging CRASH at the front of the procession. One of the musicians had dropped an instrument!

As people hurried forward to see what

116

was happening, Kirsty quickly grabbed Rachel's arm.

"It's now or never!" she exclaimed. "Everyone's looking at the musician. Let's go!"

The girls opened their lockets and sprinkled the sparkling fairy dust over themselves. Instantly, they shrank to fairy-size and felt delicate wings unfurling on their backs. Then there was a golden flash, and they were fluttering in a snowy glade in Fairyland.

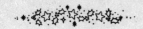

They saw Robyn immediately. She was standing beside the broken stage with Natalie the Christmas Stocking Fairy and Chrissie the Wish Fairy. They all looked very serious.

"Robyn!" called Rachel, waving to them.

She and Kirsty landed next to the fairies. They hugged Natalie and Chrissie.

"It's so nice to see you!" Kirsty exclaimed.

"All of the Christmas Fairies are gathering here," said Robyn with a smile.

She waved her hand toward the ice-skating rink. The girls could see Holly and Cheryl chatting with Paige, Stella, Gabriella, and Angelica.

"We were supposed to be putting the finishing touches on the glade," said Chrissie, giving a helpless shrug. "But we had to stop— none of our spells are working properly."

"Rachel had an idea that might help," said Kirsty.

Together, the girls explained why they thought that the snow globe might be hidden in the glade. The fairies were excited by the idea.

"But if the snow globe *is* here, wouldn't its magic have fixed the stage by now?" asked Rachel.

"I don't think so," said Robyn. "The snow globe's magic works based on

whoever is holding it."

"So the goblin who's guarding it for Jack Frost is keeping its magic from fixing the broken stage and everything else?" said Kirsty.

"Exactly," said Robyn. "So you may be right. It could still be close by!"

Rachel, Kirsty, and the Christmas Fairies started to search. They looked behind bushes, around the ice rink, and in every shadowy nook and cranny of the glade. They even flew up into the trees, in case the goblin had scrambled up

there. But there was no sign of a goblin
or the snow globe.

Rachel fluttered down and sat on a
piece of the broken stage, and Robyn
and Kirsty joined her. Rachel rested her
chin on her hand and sighed.

"Maybe I made a mistake about
the meaning of the spell," she said. "I
probably got it all wrong."

Robyn patted Rachel kindly on
the shoulder.

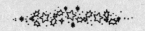

"I still think your idea made sense," she said. "Don't be upset, Rachel. You and Kirsty have been helping me so much. We've searched everywhere!"

Just then, Kirsty gave a little squeak of excitement.

"There's one place we haven't checked!" she said, waving her hand around at the pieces of rubble. "*Under the broken stage!*"

A Pinch of Pepper

The fairies looked at one another in excitement. Suddenly, they all felt absolutely sure that the goblin was somewhere under the stage! They got down on their hands and knees and peeked into the dark spaces between the broken sections of stage. But they still couldn't see anything.

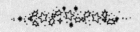

Robyn pulled out her wand and pointed it into the darkness.

"*Sneeze and sniffle, head to toes.*
Let my spell get up your nose!"

A thin stream of something black and powdery shot out of the wand and swirled into the darkness.

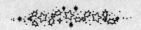

"What was that?" asked Kirsty.

"Pepper," Robyn whispered, winking at them over her shoulder.

She put a finger to her lips and then flew up and hovered over the center of the stage. Hardly daring to breathe or move, the girls listened. Seconds ticked by in silence. Then . . .

"ACHOOOOOOOOOO!"

"He's here!" Rachel exclaimed, leaping to her feet. "We found him!"

Robyn flew back to them, and they all shared a hug.

"We did it!" cried Robyn, jumping up and down. "We found my magic snow globe!"

"Yes," said Kirsty, "but how are we going to get it back?"

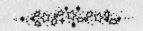

They looked at the stage again and
realized how tricky Jack Frost had been.
They couldn't fix the stage without the
snow globe, but they couldn't reach
the snow globe until the stage was fixed.

"We need to be even smaller than
fairies to get in there," said Rachel.
"Robyn, can you make us really tiny?
Maybe we can convince the goblin to
give back the snow globe."

Robyn waved her wand
in a circle around them.
A shimmering band
of golden light
appeared for a
moment, and then
all three of them
shrank until they were
no bigger than fireflies.

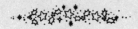

Now it was easy to get under the
stage! There were wide gaps between
the floorboards, and the three friends
swooped through easily. They flitted
around bits of broken wood and between
heavy blocks. There was a strong smell
of damp dirt, and they could feel little
bursts of icy air coming from all
directions.

"Stop!" whispered Kirsty, who was flying in front. "I can see the goblin!"

He was sitting hunched up with his back against a crooked wooden post. His teeth were chattering loudly, and a drip from his nose had frozen into a tiny icicle. He was gazing down at his bony hands.

"Let's fly around behind him and see if we can spot the snow globe," Robyn suggested softly.

Staying in the shadows, they flew carefully around the goblin until they were hovering behind his ear. There was

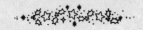

nothing on the ground next to him, but
then Rachel looked over his shoulder and
signaled to the others. Without saying a
word, she pointed down at
his hands.

The goblin
was clasping
a beautiful
crystal
globe, set
on a silver
base. Tiny
flakes of
snow whirled
around the
miniature Christmas tree inside. The star
on top of the tree seemed to glow, and
as the snow swirled around it, the globe
sparkled even more. The goblin couldn't

132

take his eyes off it.

"The snow globe seems enormous now that we're so small," whispered Robyn. "Even if we could distract the goblin from it, there's no way we could lift it."

"Then we'll just have to persuade him to come out and give it to us," said Rachel. "Come on!"

Butterfingers!

Rachel flew out in front of the goblin's face, and Kirsty and Robyn zoomed after her.

"Excuse me, goblin," said Rachel in a polite voice.

The goblin jumped in surprise and bumped his head on the stage.

"Ow!" he groaned, scowling. "That was your fault, you pesky fairy!"

"That snow globe doesn't belong to you," said Robyn.

"Who cares?" the goblin snapped, rubbing his head. "*I've* got it now."

"But you're ruining Christmas parties everywhere by keeping it here," said Kirsty. "And it doesn't look like you're having much fun, either."

"It's cold and damp," said the goblin, glaring at her. "I love it!"

"Oh dear," said Rachel with a sigh. "Listen, Mr. Goblin, it's almost Christmas. Don't you want to do something kind for a change?"

The goblin's eyes opened wide, and for a moment Rachel felt hopeful. But then . . .

"NO!" he bellowed.

Rachel and Kirsty glanced at each other sadly.

"While we're under here, we're too small to take the snow globe back," Kirsty whispered. "We need to get the goblin out into the glade. Maybe then we'll figure out a way to get the snow globe from him."

"But how are we going to get him out of here?" asked Rachel. "He says he likes

it down here."

"Exactly!" Robyn exclaimed. "He says he likes it because it's cold and miserable—so let's change that!"

She waved her wand, and suddenly the icy gusts of wind stopped. Instead, the girls felt a warm breeze ruffle their hair. It smelled like apple blossoms!

"BLECH!" grumbled the goblin. "That stinks!"

The air grew warmer, and sweat began to pour down his face. Suddenly, all the broken slabs and bricks nearby turned a delicate shade of pink, and pictures of fluffy kittens and puppies appeared on them.

"YUCK!" yelled the goblin. "What's happening? This is awful!"

Rachel and Kirsty covered their mouths, trying to stifle their giggles.

Finally, tinkling ballet music began to play, and the goblin leaped to his feet.

"I'm not staying here!" he wailed. "This is torture!"

He scrambled past the broken blocks, shoving them out of his way and sending bricks and slabs of wood flying in all directions. He burst out through a thin plank of wood and jumped on top of the rubble.

"Quick, follow him!" cried Kirsty.

The friends whizzed out behind the goblin as fast as they could, and Robyn instantly returned them to fairy-size.

The goblin was scrambling and stumbling across the rubble. He was holding the snow globe in one hand, but it kept almost slipping out of his grasp as he wobbled along.

"He's going to drop it!" cried Robyn in a horrified voice. "If it breaks, Christmas parties will be ruined for good!"

The three fairies fluttered around the goblin's head in a panic.

"Please put the snow globe down," Robyn pleaded.

"Leave me alone!" shouted the goblin.

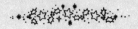

"Just let us have the snow globe!"
Rachel cried. "It belongs to Robyn."

Suddenly, there was a blinding flash
of lightning, and Jack Frost appeared in
front of them.

"Where's my special snow globe?" he
screeched angrily.

Shocked, the goblin flung up his hands—
and the snow globe flew into the air!

"NO!" yelled Kirsty and Rachel.

"BUTTERFINGERS!" cried Jack
Frost loudly.

"HELP!" the goblin squawked.

Robyn zoomed after the snow globe, as
it arched through the air and then began
to fall. It hurtled toward the ground,
faster and faster. Robyn raced across
the glade as the others held their breath.
Robyn dived for the snow globe with her
hands outstretched . . .

"YES!" cheered Rachel and Kirsty.

The Christmas Party Fairy had caught her snow globe just in time! Jack Frost snarled and grabbed the goblin's ear.

"You numbskull!" he roared. "Now look what you've done!"

"It was those pesky fairies!" wailed the goblin.

"I'll get my revenge!" Jack Frost declared angrily.

"Not this Christmas, Jack Frost!" said Robyn, folding her arms across her chest.

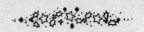

Grumbling loudly, Jack Frost and the goblin disappeared in a flash of blue lightning. Robyn turned to the girls and held up the snow globe with a beaming smile. It had returned to fairy-size, and it was giving out a warm, Christmassy glow. Robyn shook it, and it sparkled as the snow inside swirled.

"I wish for everything to return to normal," she said.

There was a loud whooshing sound,
and the pieces of rubble around them
started to tremble.

In a swirl of sparkles, they were
whisked up into the air—and turned into
a stage that looked as good as new!

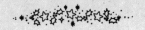

"We did it!" Kirsty exclaimed, twirling into the air in delight. "Christmas parties are saved!"

"All thanks to you!" said Robyn, hugging the girls. "But it's getting late. We have to work fast to get everything ready in time for the party!"

Parties Galore!

Rachel, Kirsty, and all of the Christmas Fairies worked very hard to make sure that the party would be perfect. When the guests arrived, the glade looked enchanting! There were tiny sparkling lights in every tree, and beautifully wrapped presents hanging from the branches.

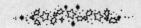

Rachel and Kirsty were thrilled to see so many familiar faces. The Rainbow Fairies swooped down to greet them with hugs and kisses. The Pet Fairies hurried over to say hello, and crowds of other fairy friends waved, blew kisses, and wished them a merry Christmas.

The performances were wonderful.
First, there was amazing ballroom, salsa,
and ballet dancing. Then there was a
wonderful caroling concert from the
Music Fairies . . . and the goblins!

"My hands hurt from clapping so
hard!" said Kirsty, taking a sip of her
delicious blackberry-dew tea.

Rachel smiled and then gasped as a murmur went through the crowd of fairies. Jack Frost had walked into the glade!

"He looks mad," whispered Kirsty.

The fairies parted to let him through, and he stalked toward the stage. He was glaring at the goblins, whose knees started knocking together.

Robyn stepped into his path. With one hand she held up her snow globe and shook it, and with her other hand she

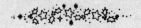

offered Jack Frost a mug of hot berry
juice. A smile flickered around his thin
lips, and he took the mug.

"That's the Christmas party spirit
weaving its magic!" said Rachel.

Jack Frost sat down in a front-row seat
as Isabelle and Isla stepped onto the ice
rink for the next performance. It was
going to be a magnificent show!

Robyn's party was everything the perfect Christmas party should be. There was wonderful food, plenty of dancing and singing, and lots of laughter. At last, with streamers dangling from their hair and music ringing in their ears, it was time for the girls to go home. Robyn tapped their lockets with her wand to fill them with fairy dust again. Then she hugged both girls tightly.

"Thank you for helping me save Christmas parties everywhere," she said. "You're fantastic friends!"

"We're glad we could help," said Rachel. "And thank you for inviting us to an amazing party!"

"Yours is going to be just as amazing," said Robyn. "And it's time you went back to it! Good-bye, girls, and merry Christmas!"

The sound of fairy laughter and music was suddenly replaced by the voices of the Wetherbury carol singers. The girls were back in the human world, and not a moment had passed since they had left.

Rachel and Kirsty were still at the back of the procession, but now the lanterns were all glowing and the musicians were playing perfectly.

"Come on, girls!" called Mrs. Tate, glancing back at them. "We're almost at the Town Hall!"

Everyone in Wetherbury agreed that it was the best Christmas party ever. The ballerinas had never danced so perfectly, the carol singers had never sounded so sweet, and the music had never been so festive. The party guests clapped and cheered, and the girls' hands ached from joining in, after all the applause at the fairy party earlier.

When everyone sat down to enjoy the feast, Kirsty and Rachel had fun trying all the different cakes, pies, sandwiches, and desserts that filled the tables. They didn't even notice how late it was until the clock struck midnight. On the first BONG, the doors of the Town Hall flew wide open.

"Ho, ho, ho!" said a merry voice.

"It's Santa Claus!" cried Kirsty in delight.

"And he's got a sackful of presents!" Rachel added with an excited giggle.

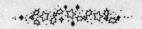

As Santa Claus made his way around the hall, handing out presents and shaking hands, Rachel turned to Kirsty and gave her a hug.

"Thank you for inviting me to spend Christmas with you," she said. "I love the adventures we have together!"

"Me, too," said Kirsty, hugging her back. "I'm so lucky to have such an amazing best friend. Today has been the best Christmas Eve *ever*!"

The two friends grinned at each other. This Christmas had been more than the best—it had been absolutely magical!

RAINBOW magic

SPECIAL EDITION

Rachel and Kirsty have found
Robyn's missing magic objects.
Now it's time for them to help

Michelle
the Winter Wonderland Fairy!

Join their next adventure in this
special sneak peek . . .

The Frosty Ferry

"It was so nice of your mom to invite me on this trip," Rachel Walker said to her best friend, Kirsty Tate. She looked out at the blue waves churning around the ferry and took a deep breath.

"The trip was my mom's prize for winning a painting contest. It was for her favorite travel website," Kirsty explained. Kirsty was proud of her mom. Mrs. Tate's oil painting was beautiful—a stunning close-up of the details of a deep green pine-tree branch, dusted with crystal-white snow. The painting's background was of the serene landscape of snow-covered hills. "I've never been to Snowbound Island before, and this is the weekend of their famous Winter Wonder Festival."

"I've never been to a winter resort, either, but the photos on the website looked almost exactly like your mom's painting," Rachel said.

"Maybe that's why she won!" Kirsty mused. "You know, my mom said she was

looking forward to sleeping in and having breakfast in bed, but I'm just excited to get out in the snow."

"I know. We haven't had any snow at home at all." Even though it was well into December and almost time to celebrate the winter holidays, the weather had been dreary and rainy.

"My dad checked the forecast. They've had tons of snow on the island," Kirsty said.

"I think he was right," Rachel said, pointing.

Kirsty turned to see the sweetest tuft of land. It looked almost like a glacier, rising right out of the crashing waves. From this distance, they could see the ski slopes, treeless paths that curved down the steep mountainside. There

was also a large, wooden building with smoke puffing out of the chimney. Kirsty guessed it must be the lodge. As the ferry chugged closer, the water became choppier. Rachel lost her balance, and both girls laughed as they grabbed the railing.

"I can't wait!" Rachel admitted. "I don't know if I want to ski or skate first."

"Or snowshoe or sled," Kirsty added, and then paused. "On second thought, sledding is my first choice. Definitely."

Just then, a door to the boat's cabin opened, and Mr. Tate poked his head outside. "Brrrrr," he said as the wind gusted by. "The captain said the sea is too cold and unruly, so you two need to come inside. There are huge waves and chunks of ice. It's getting dangerous."

SPECIAL EDITION

Which Magical Fairies Have You Met?

- ❏ Joy the Summer Vacation Fairy
- ❏ Holly the Christmas Fairy
- ❏ Kylie the Carnival Fairy
- ❏ Stella the Star Fairy
- ❏ Shannon the Ocean Fairy
- ❏ Trixie the Halloween Fairy
- ❏ Gabriella the Snow Kingdom Fairy
- ❏ Juliet the Valentine Fairy
- ❏ Mia the Bridesmaid Fairy
- ❏ Flora the Dress-Up Fairy
- ❏ Paige the Christmas Play Fairy
- ❏ Emma the Easter Fairy
- ❏ Cara the Camp Fairy
- ❏ Destiny the Rock Star Fairy
- ❏ Belle the Birthday Fairy
- ❏ Olympia the Games Fairy
- ❏ Selena the Sleepover Fairy

- ❏ Cheryl the Christmas Tree Fairy
- ❏ Florence the Friendship Fairy
- ❏ Lindsay the Luck Fairy
- ❏ Brianna the Tooth Fairy
- ❏ Autumn the Falling Leaves Fairy
- ❏ Keira the Movie Star Fairy
- ❏ Addison the April Fool's Day Fairy
- ❏ Bailey the Babysitter Fairy
- ❏ Natalie the Christmas Stocking Fairy
- ❏ Lila and Myla the Twins Fairies
- ❏ Chelsea the Congratulations Fairy
- ❏ Carly the School Fairy
- ❏ Angelica the Angel Fairy
- ❏ Blossom the Flower Girl Fairy
- ❏ Skyler the Fireworks Fairy
- ❏ Giselle the Christmas Ballet Fairy
- ❏ Alicia the Snow Queen Fairy

SCHOLASTIC
Find all of your favorite fairy friends at
scholastic.com/rainbowmagic

3 stories in each one!

HIT entertainment

RMSPECIAL20

OCT 2018

RAINBOW
magic

Which Magical Fairies Have You Met?

- ☐ The Rainbow Fairies
- ☐ The Weather Fairies
- ☐ The Jewel Fairies
- ☐ The Pet Fairies
- ☐ The Sports Fairies
- ☐ The Ocean Fairies
- ☐ The Princess Fairies
- ☐ The Superstar Fairies
- ☐ The Fashion Fairies
- ☐ The Sugar & Spice Fairies
- ☐ The Earth Fairies
- ☐ The Magical Crafts Fairies
- ☐ The Baby Animal Rescue Fairies
- ☐ The Fairy Tale Fairies
- ☐ The School Day Fairies
- ☐ The Storybook Fairies
- ☐ The Friendship Fairies

 SCHOLASTIC

HiT entertainment

Find all of your favorite fairy friends at
scholastic.com/rainbowmagic

RMFAIRY17